This book is dedicated with heartfelt thanks to
Mick Moore for all his help and encouragement.

With special thanks to:
Mark Gillmon and Hiab
Charlie Turner and Fender
James Menhinick and Pickup

And thanks to:
Timmy Dufort
Ryan Nethercot
Cornish Birds of Prey Centre

www.veronicalamond.com

Landy's New Home

Written and illustrated by
Veronica Lamond

It was a very hot day.
Landy and Molly dozed in the sunshine.

But Jack had big plans.

"Ouch! You're so hot, Landy," he said, "we could fry eggs on your bonnet!"

Jack took off Landy's door tops and rolled up his canvas.

"That should cool you down," he said.

"Aaah, that's better," said Landy.

"Let's go to Mark's Yard," said Jack.
Molly jumped onto her seat and off they went.
As they drove down the lane, Katy passed by
on her bicycle.

"BEEP! BEEP!" said Landy.

Mark's Yard was full of all sorts of things —
bricks and slate,
iron and wood,
stone and steel.

Landy watched the crane lifting timber, while Jack hunted for planks and corrugated iron.

"This lot will keep you busy," said Mark, as he helped Jack load everything into Landy.

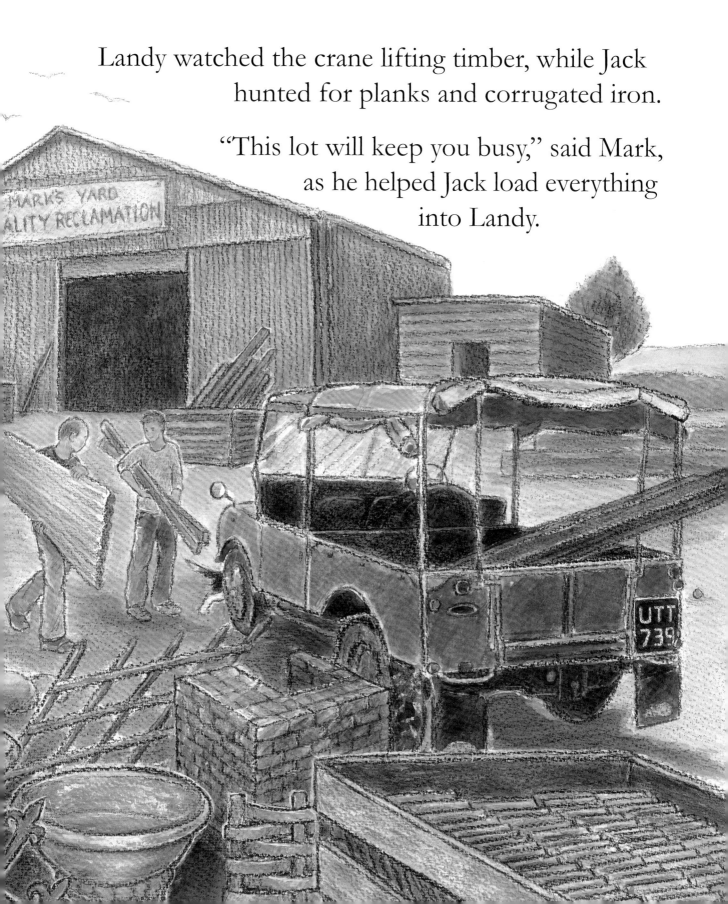

Back at home,
Jack cleared
and dug
the ground.

He measured
and cut the wood.

Then he hammered the nails BANG! BANG! BANG!

Landy watched and
dreamed of what Jack
might be making for him.

But Jack built a little house,

then another one…

then three more!

The wood was all used up and Jack put away his tools.

Landy felt very upset.
"I can't fit into any of those houses!" he said.
"How could Jack forget me?"

The next day they drove to Florrie's
to pick up some new friends.

The goats weren't easy to catch!

"Those geese look like trouble!" said Landy.

James and Pickup dropped off Spotty and Dotty and some hay for the animals.

"Ha! ha! This is a silly little farm!" honked Pickup.

"Beeeep!" said Landy
"Hissss!" said the geese.
"Meeeh!" said the goats.

"Woof! Woof!" barked Molly.

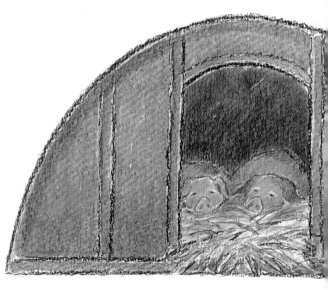

Everyone found their
new homes

and settled down
for the night.

"Night night, Molly,"
said Jack.

"Woof!" said Molly.

Landy watched as the light went out.

Clouds gathered in the dark sky.
Lightning flashed, thunder crashed
and the rain poured down.

Landy stood all alone, getting wetter
and wetter. Rain soaked his seats
and flooded his floor.

He felt miserable.

The next morning, Jack was up bright and early.

He jumped into Landy,

but jumped straight out again.

His trousers were soaking wet!

Landy laughed…

and laughed…

and laughed!

Then Dan and Fender drove in through the gate.
They were loaded up with wood.

"We've come to help Jack build your new home Landy,"
said Fender, "he hasn't forgotten you!"

"Come on, Dan," said Jack, "we'd better get started. Landy's not happy with me!"

Landy and Fender had fun with all the animals.

Jack and Dan worked
all day long.

By evening the job was done.
Jack reversed Landy into his new home.
Everyone came to look.

"BEEP! BEEP! Thank you very much!" said Landy.
"This is the best home in the whole wide world!"

Books in the Landybook series

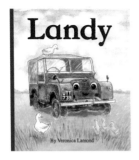   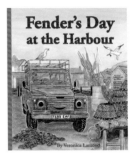

Also by
Veronica Lamond

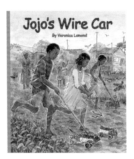

First published in September 2010 by Veronica Lamond

The author asserts her moral rights to be recognised as the author and illustrator of this work. All rights reserved.

This edition published in 2015 by Struik Nature (an imprint of Penguin Random House South Africa (Pty) Ltd)
Reg. No. 1953/000441/07
The Estuaries, No. 4, Oxbow Crescent (off Century Avenue), Century City, 7441 South Africa
PO Box 1144, Cape Town, 8000 South Africa

10 9 8 7 6 5 4 3 2

Printed and bound in China by C&C Offset Printing Co., Ltd

ISBN 978 1 77584 290 3